Marta Perry

"Marta Perry illuminates the differences between
the Amish community and the larger society with an
obvious care and respect for ways and beliefs....
She weaves these differences into the story
with a deft hand, drawing the reader into a suspenseful,
continually moving plot."
—*Fresh Fiction* on *Murder in Plain Sight*

"*Leah's Choice,* by Marta Perry, is a knowing
and careful look into Amish culture and faith.
A truly enjoyable reading experience."
—Angela Hunt, *New York Times* bestselling author
of *Let Darkness Come*

"*Leah's Choice* takes us into the heart of Amish country
and the Pennsylvania Dutch and shows us the struggles
of the Amish community as the outside world continues
to clash with the Plain ways. This is a story of grace
and servitude as well as a story of difficult choices and
heartbreaking realities. It touched my heart. I think the
world of Amish fiction has found a new champion."
—Lenora Worth, author of *Code of Honor*

"Marta Perry delivers a strong story of tension, fear and
trepidation. *Season of Secrets* (4.5 stars) is an excellent
mystery that's certain to keep you in constant suspense.
While love is a powerful entity in this story,
danger is never too far behind."
—*RT Book Reviews*, Top Pick

"In this beautifully told tale, Marta Perry writes with
the gentle cadence and rich detail of someone who
understands the Amish well. *Leah's Choice*
kept me reading long into the night."
—Linda Goodnight, author of *Finding Her Way Home*